Track a T-Rex

Written by Helen Dineen

Illustrated by Barry Ablett

Collins

This is Stan. He is a T-Rex fossil.

3

Fossils help experts get the facts.

the dig

They brush dust and grit from
T-Rex fossils.

Stomp, crash, smash! T-Rex is on the hunt.

Stomp Power

★ ★ ★

Big T-Rex footprints in the forest.

T-Rex sniffs the air. He tracks down food.

Smell Power

★ ★ ★

A talent
for smell
helps T-Rex.

9

T-Rex is strong. He grips, twists and turns.

Chomp Power

Sharp teeth grab and strip flesh.

Now T-Rex has lunch.
What a strong hunter!

Dung Power

★★★★★

There are bits
of skeleton
in T-Rex dung!

Track T-Rex

After reading

Letters and Sounds: Phase 4

Word count: 100

Focus on adjacent consonants with short vowel phonemes, e.g. *strong*.

Common exception words: he, of, the, I, was, they, what, there, are

Curriculum links (EYFS): Understanding the world

Curriculum links (National Curriculum, Year 1): Science: Animals, including humans

Early learning goals: Reading: read and understand simple sentences; use phonic knowledge to decode regular words and read them aloud accurately; read some common irregular words

National Curriculum learning objectives: Reading/word reading: read accurately by blending sounds in unfamiliar words containing GPCs that have been taught; Reading/comprehension: understand both the books they can already read accurately and fluently and those they listen to by checking that the text makes sense to them as they read, and correcting inaccurate reading

Developing fluency

- Your child may enjoy hearing you read the text.
- Ask your child to read the main text, making sure they notice the commas and full stops, whilst you read the labels, speech bubbles and fact boxes.

Phonic practice

- Practise reading words that contain adjacent consonants. Encourage your child to sound out and blend the following:

  sniffs   smell   tracks   helps   grips

- Focus on double syllable words, breaking the words into "chunks" if necessary as they read.

  power   hunter   talent   footprints

Extending vocabulary

- Take turns to point to a word and challenge each other to explain the meaning of the word, or to suggest a synonym (word or words with a similar meaning).
- Begin by pointing to **experts** on page 4, saying: What does this mean? (e.g. people who know a lot about something)